For Susan…who helps me see
the magic in the moon.
Love, F.F.

the Story of PUMPKIN

Written & Illustrated by
Frank Fiorello

10 9 8 7 6 5 4 3 2

For information, please address:
Frank Fiorello,
3178 Route 173,
Caledonia, IL 61011
Phone 815/765-2587

Library of Congress
Catalog Card Number: 97-90377

Paperback ISBN: 0-9646300-2-8

Come with me, far into October, near the end of fall.

When butterflies are on the wing.

And fuzzy caterpillars munch
on the last leaves of Indian Summer.

Where bushy tailed squirrels scamper to hide food for the coming winter.

And field mice ready their nest.

The red fox silently awaits the coming cold, as ducks head south in search of warm weather and open water.

Soon, Jack Frost will signal
the cold north winds to come howling
over the plains, onto the Pumpkin Patch.

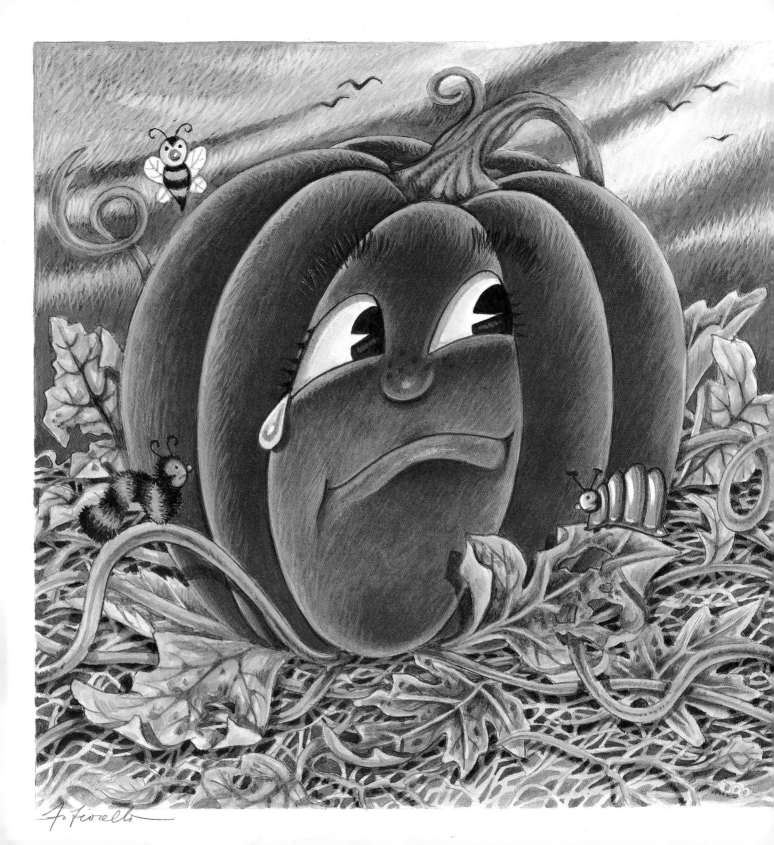

Where sits the
littlest
PUMPKIN.

Halloween has
come and
PUMPKIN
was not
picked to
be a
Jack-O-Lantern.

He will have to spend winter alone in the Patch.

In November,
around Thanksgiving, winter snows come calling.

Now PUMPKIN will settle in
for a long winter's nap.

As the north wind blows colder, PUMPKIN will shrink and shrivel into the ground, along with his seeds.

Most of PUMPKIN'S seeds will be eaten by hungry field mice.

But some of the seeds will nestle into the good earth where they will be protected by snow cover and PUMPKIN'S shrinking walls.

The
littlest
PUMPKIN
will sleep
through
December…

Through January...

$\mathbf{A}$nd through February...

Until the melting snows of March nourish the seeds of sleeping PUMPKIN.

Finally, spring arrives with chirping birds and colorful blossoms bursting forth.

Soon PUMPKIN'S seeds
will take root into
the soft ground.

And the first tender sprouts of PUMPKIN will emerge.

Green leaves will take shape
and twisting vines will grow.

T

hen yellow
flowers will
appear, stretching
towards the sun,
inviting buzzing bees
to help with
pollination.

PUMPKIN will begin again as a small green ball.

Growing bigger
and
bigger.

Warmed
by the
autumn
sun,

PUMPKIN will slowly turn orange.

This time
a happy
family decides
to take
PUMPKIN
home

To become a proud Jack-O-Lantern.